KU-781-540

# I Won't Go

# To China

UWE, Bristol
AR-52209
2 4 MAY 2012
ACE
Library Services

## Enda Wyley

Illustrated by Marie Thorhauge
of The Cartoon Saloon

THE O'BRIEN PRESS
DUBLIN

*Dedication*
For Adam Zheng
with special thanks to Lisa and Yi Zheng.

ENDA WYLEY is a poet and a children's writer. Her children's books are: *The Silver Notebook*, *Boo and Bear*.

First published 2009 by The O'Brien Press Ltd,
12 Terenure Road East, Rathgar, Dublin 6, Ireland.
Tel: +353 1 4923333; Fax: +353 1 4922777
E-mail: books@obrien.ie
Website: www.obrien.ie

ISBN: 978-1-84717-159-7

Copyright for text © Enda Wyley 2009

Copyright for typesetting, design, and editing © The O'Brien Press Ltd.

Kindly supported by

The Department of
**Arts, Sport and Tourism**
An Roinn
**Ealaíon, Spóirt agus Turasóireachta**

All rights reserved. No part of this publication may be reproduced or utilised in any form or by any means, electronic or mechanical, including photocopying, recording or in any information storage and retrieval system, without permission in writing from the publisher.

British Library Cataloguing-in-Publication Data
A catalogue record for this title is available from the British Library

1 2 3 4 5 6 7 8 9 10
09 10 11 12 13 14 15

Printed and bound in Poland by Białostockie Zakłady Graficzne S.A.
The paper in this book is produced using pulp from managed forests.

新年快乐

*Xin Nian Kuai Le!*

Happy New Year!

Chang-ming was delighted. He had been chosen to play on the school football team against their great rivals, Grove school, in a few weeks. He couldn't wait to tell his mum and dad.

But their faces fell.

'Chang-ming,' said his mother, Mei Li, 'we will be in China then, don't you remember?'

Chang-ming was going on his first ever visit to his
grandma in China for the Chinese New Year.

'No! I can't go! I must play for the shool.'

'But we have the plane tickets. And Grandma is
expecting us,' said his dad, Tao.

Suddenly Chang-ming was the unhappiest boy around.

'I won't go to China!' he said.

After that, Chang-ming decided he hated being Chinese.

'My name's silly,' he told his mother next day after school. 'Wang Chang-ming. What kind of a name is that?' he said. 'I *hate* when the teacher puts Wang first. That's my last name. It should *be* last!'

'But that's how it is in Chinese,' his mum sighed.

'I know. But the others don't have their second names coming first. It's stupid.'

Mei Li shook her head. She looked sad. She was very proud of being Chinese. She and Tao had moved to Ireland from China. When their little son was born, a full moon shone brightly in the night sky.

'Look,' said Tao, 'our baby's special moon.'

They called him Chang-ming because the name means 'Forever Bright'.

'Just like that beautiful moon,' Mei Li said.

But Chang-ming didn't want to be called Forever Bright.

He wanted to be called Conor or Barry or Jack – something

*normal.*

'And I'm *not* going to talk to Grandma when she rings!'

Chang-ming said. 'Even if she *is* calling all the way

from China!'

Chang-ming's grandmother lived in Beijing. She rang every month. She had never seen Chang-ming, except in photographs. Mei Li sent her photographs every few months. So Grandma knew all about Chang-ming.

Chang-ming knew all about his grandmother too, and the family had lots of photographs of her.

He could talk to her on the phone because Chang-ming could speak Chinese – that's what they spoke at home.

'Anyway, why should I care about someone I have never met?' Chang-ming said to his parents next day.

'Chang-ming, you must honour your grandmother,' his father said. 'She's old and wise. She knows lots of things you don't know yet.'

Chang-ming didn't know what to say to that. 'But it's a great honour to play for the school,' he said finally. 'The teacher said that to the whole class.'

Poor Chang-ming. He was so sad.

UWE LIBRARY SERVICES

His parents were sad too. They were thrilled that their boy had been chosen for the team. But they couldn't change their plane tickets, and Grandma had been looking forward to their visit for ages. They couldn't disappoint her.

'I know you're disappointed, Chang-ming,' said his father. 'But a trip to China has to be more exciting than a football match!'

*More exciting than a football match!* This football match was the most important thing in the whole world.

'I won't go to China,' Chang-ming said. 'I'm staying here.'

Mei Li decided the best thing to do was to talk to Chang-ming's teacher, Mrs Pepper, one day after school.

His mother tried to explain to Mrs Pepper that Chang-ming was unhappy. He really wanted to play for the school. He did not want to go to see his grandmother in China. He was very troublesome at home. She was very upset. But they could not change their plans.

The teacher listened.

'Poor Chang-ming,' Mrs Pepper said finally. 'But I think I may be able to help. In my class we love to talk about how people live in different places,' she explained. 'Revati is from India, and her mum came in and cooked an Indian curry for us. It was delicious. Roisin's father is from the Aran Islands, and he played the tin whistle for us. The children loved it! Now they all want to learn to play it.'

'Oh!' said Mei Li. 'I did not know.'

'Now,' Mrs Pepper said, 'please make sure Chang-ming is late tomorrow morning.'

Mei Li was delighted. The teacher would help. Her little boy would be happy again. She sang all the way home. And at dinner when Chang-ming wouldn't eat his noodles and demanded pizza, she just laughed.

The next day Chang-ming was late for school. And when he got there, everyone was delighted to see him.

'Chang-ming,' announced Mrs Pepper, 'you have a very special task. You must do it for the whole class. Isn't that right, children?' They all agreed.

'Now,' she explained, 'you were chosen to represent the school in the football match. But you will be in China.'

Chang-ming hung his head.

'So,' said Mrs Pepper, 'you must represent the school in China instead. You will arrive just in time for the Chinese New Year. It takes place at the start of February this year, and is very different from our New Year. We want to know all about it. So, we are giving you this and this.'

She held out two things: the school camera and a large notebook. It was a very special notebook; it had a red cloth cover.

When they arrived in Beijing, twelve hours later, Chang-ming felt tired and hot. Soon they left the airport and Chang-ming stared around. There were people everywhere. They were rushing to catch trains and buses and planes. They were all going home for the New Year.

'It's like Christmas back in Ireland,' said Chang-ming. 'Only worse.'

'We're lucky,' his dad said. 'Grandma lives right here in the city.' They got on a bus to go to her street.

Chang-ming had never seen anything like Beijing. There were wide streets with lots of traffic lanes, and apartment blocks over forty floors high. Far off in the distance, he spotted temples and towers and old walls. There were bicycles everywhere.

Chang-ming couldn't stop taking photographs.

Soon the bus stopped in the centre of the city.

'Grandma lives down this old narrow street called Mao Er Hutong – that means "Cat's Ear Lane" – because the alley is so small,' Tao explained. 'Many of the old houses have been knocked down to make room for office blocks and apartments, but your Grandma still lives in one.'

Chang-ming saw a pair of stone lions standing at a bright red gate. Mei Li turned the copper rings on the gate and it opened into a courtyard full of plants and flowers, with four rooms facing out onto it.

23

UWE LIBRARY SERVICES

'The courtyard keeps everyone safe from the terrible winter winds and the dust storms of spring,' Mei Li said.

A door was flung open and there was Chang-ming's grandmother. She had been busy sweeping all the rooms to clean away bad luck for New Year. When she saw her family, she dropped the brush.

'Chang-ming! My only grandson!' she cried. Her old face burst into a huge smile. She threw her arms around Chang-ming and he felt strange and happy.

The days sped by. Chang-ming helped his dad with the preparations for New Year. On each side of Grandma's front door they hung two large pieces of red paper with good luck greetings printed on them.

Chang-ming also went to have his hair cut because Grandma said that this would bring him good luck. As his hair fell to the floor, Chang-ming closed his eyes and made a special wish: *I wish we will beat Grove school and I can play in the next match!*

Grandma had decided to hold a special party. The house was filled with beautiful flowers and incense was lit. Grandma and Mei Li cooked delicious fish and chicken for everyone. They also made dumplings stuffed with pork and vegetables. Some of the dumplings had coins hidden in them and others had dates.

'If you get a dumpling with a coin, you will be wealthy,' Grandma explained to Chang-ming.

'And the dates mean you will be lucky,' said Mei Li.

They had all bought new Chinese clothes for the party.

'Can I take them home to Dublin?' Chang-ming asked.

'Of course,' Grandma said.

'Tell all your class that Chinese people wear something red at New Year because red keeps sadness away,' explained Grandma. 'That's why I got you red socks! And will I let you into a secret, Chang-ming?' She winked. 'I am wearing red underwear for good luck and happiness. But don't tell your friends that!'

Chang-ming giggled. He most certainly *would* tell them. He even drew a picture of her in the big notebook wearing only her underwear! He didn't show it to her, of course.

The party was wonderful. It was midnight when everyone began to eat the dumplings. Chang-ming had never been up so late.

But soon, he felt his eyes close, and he crept into bed to the sounds of chattering and fire-crackers popping. The grown-ups stayed up all night to welcome in the New Year. In the days that followed New Year, there was lots to do.

On the first day, Chang-ming was given a red envelope with money inside to bring him good luck. On the second day, everyone prayed to their ancestors. It was also the Birthday of Dogs, and Grandma told Chang-ming to be very kind to any dog he saw.

But the best day of all was the fifteenth day. People gathered in Grandma's house to share small, round, sweet dumplings, with surprises inside. Then Chang-ming went outside with Grandma to help light lots of candles in the street.

'The candles will bring lost spirits home,' Grandma said.

Then they all held lanterns, with candles inside, and walked through the streets and parks together. It was a wonderful lantern festival.

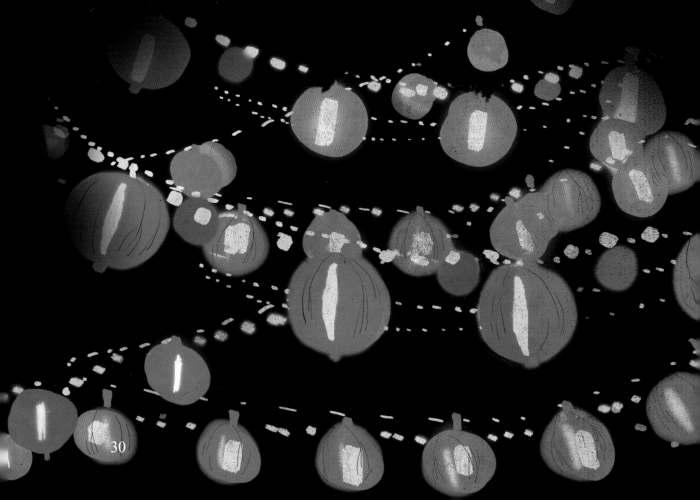

Chang-ming heard loud drums and the crash of cymbals. A huge Chinese dragon, painted in bright colours, danced down the street, and everyone cheered.

'And we have good news for you, Chang-ming!' Mei Li roared over the noise. 'The school team beat the Grove! And Mrs Pepper said you are to play in the next game!'

'Yippee!' Chang-ming shrieked. His wish had come true. 'Now I am an Expert Reporter *and* a footballer!'

He had millions of photographs of interesting things and his notebook was full of notes and drawings.

He looked at his parents. 'I'm glad to be Chinese,' he told them. 'This is great.'

Mei Li and Tao smiled. Chang-ming was happy again.

It was getting dark and the lanterns made the streets glow orange. Chang-ming felt his heart swell with happiness. Just then his grandma put her arms around him. She must have been feeling the same way.

'*Xin Nian Kuai Le!*' she said. 'Happy New Year, my dearest grandson!'

MARS.

CRETE

EGYPT

FRANCE

EIRE

RUSSIA

SIERRA LEONE

BRAZIL

IRAQ

NIGERIA

CZECH
REPUBLIC

THAILAND

GREECE

GERMANY.

CANADA.

POLAND

USA
D.